THE MASK™ IN

SCHOOL SPIRITS

By
Rick Geary

The Mask™ in School Spirits

Colors by Chris Chalenor

Publication Design by Teena Gores

Edited by Lynn Adair

The Mask™ created by Mike Richardson

THE MASK™ IN SCHOOL SPIRITS

Published by Dark Horse Comics, Inc.
10956 SE Main Street
Milwaukie, Oregon 97222

ISBN: 1-56971-121-6

First Edition: September 1995

2 4 6 8 10 9 7 5 3 1

ust when things start to get really exciting, summer vacation's over and it's back to school . . . my least favorite place to be.

I usually walk home with my friend Dallas. That's when we make our own fun. Sometimes when we're on an adventure, Dallas gets a little scared, but that's just because he's a grade behind me.

Dallas and I like to walk past the old school on Walnut Street. It closed down a long time ago and everyone says it's haunted. There's this one story about Mrs. Beasley, the school nurse whose spirit still roams the halls.

Last week, we ran into Delbert and Kendall, who are one grade ahead of me. They're okay, but they love to pull pranks on us younger kids.

"**N**urse Beasley, that's nothing!" said Delbert. Then he told us about the school's last principal, Mr. Strong, who didn't like kids at all. With the help of Russ the custodian, Mr. Strong forced all of the "problem students" into the basement and bolted the door.

"Oh, no!" cried Dallas.

Before long, Delbert and Kendall dared us to sneak into the old place the next day, after school. I knew they'd try to pull something.

Dallas and I needed a plan.

hat night, I dropped by my Uncle Stanley's. He went to the old grade school when he was a kid. I was hoping he knew of a secret passage or two.

But Uncle Stanley was too busy preparing himself for a *big date* to pay much attention to me and my questions. So, after a while, I slipped away with his treasured secret possession — the mask!

endall and Delbert were waiting for us the next afternoon. We crawled through an opening in the fence. I could tell Dallas was already nervous.

"Stay cool," I whispered, "we have an edge . . . and it's in my backpack!"

Inside, we peered down the main hallway and imagined the horror and pain endured by kids back in the old days.

"They had no computers or video games," Kendall hissed, "and sometimes they were even chained to their desks!"

 poked my head into the first classroom.

"What happened here?" I asked. But when I turned around, my friends had vanished! *I'll get them*, I said to myself. I reached into my backpack when suddenly, there was this horrible sound!

A terrible wail was coming from one of the desks . . .

When I opened the lid, out flew the grateful spirit of an old-time student.

"Thanks, kid," he said, "I've been in there for forty years!"

Maybe I should have said *you're welcome*, but who says you've got to be polite to ghosts?!

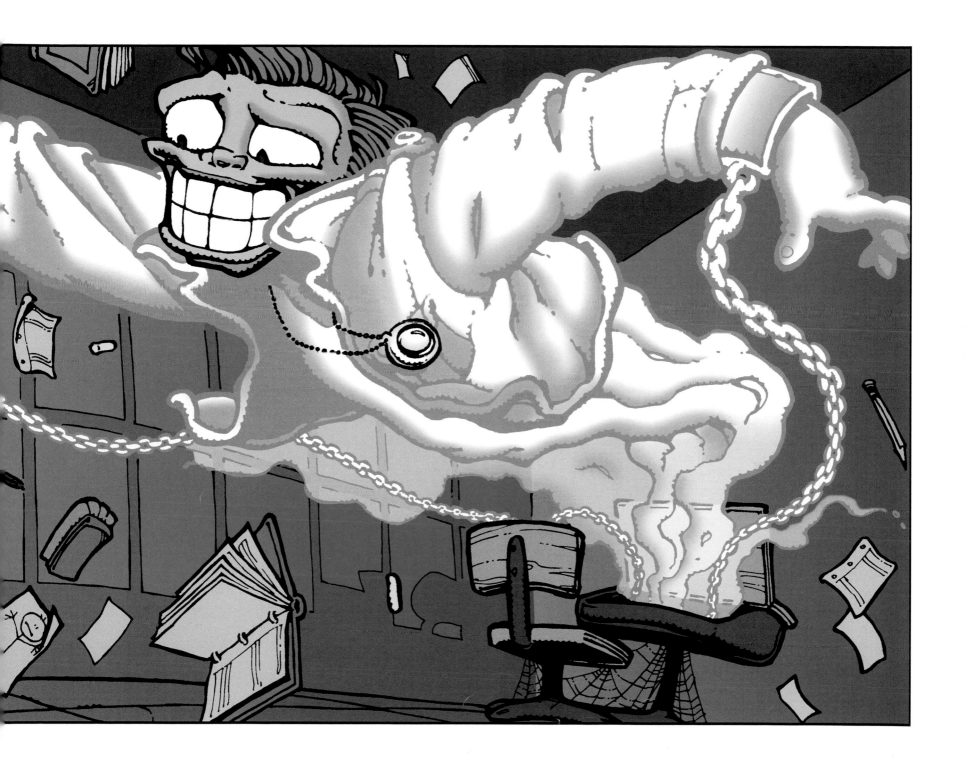

ut in the hall, I ran smack into Delbert and Kendall, who were running in the other direction. Strange lights and noises were coming from all around us.

"Maybe this place really is haunted," whimpered Delbert, "and where's Dallas?"

"He just couldn't take the heat, I guess," said Kendall through chattering teeth.

We called out Dallas' name again and again. The only answer was a chilling voice from around the corner saying, "Boys, boys . . . *Do calm down*!"

 knew who it was right away . . . Nurse Beasley, with her tray of rotting medicines.

"Come into my office," she called, "you look like you need a sedative!"

Never did three healthier kids run quite so fast. By this time, we just wanted to find the nearest exit. But before we could . . .

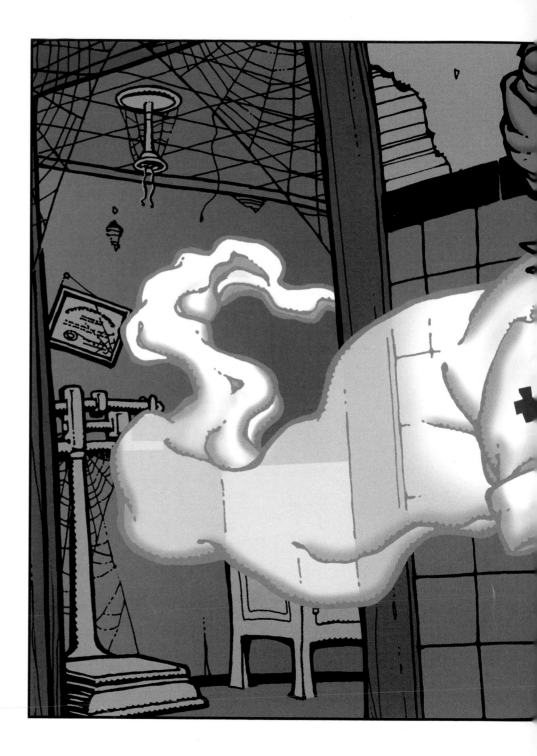

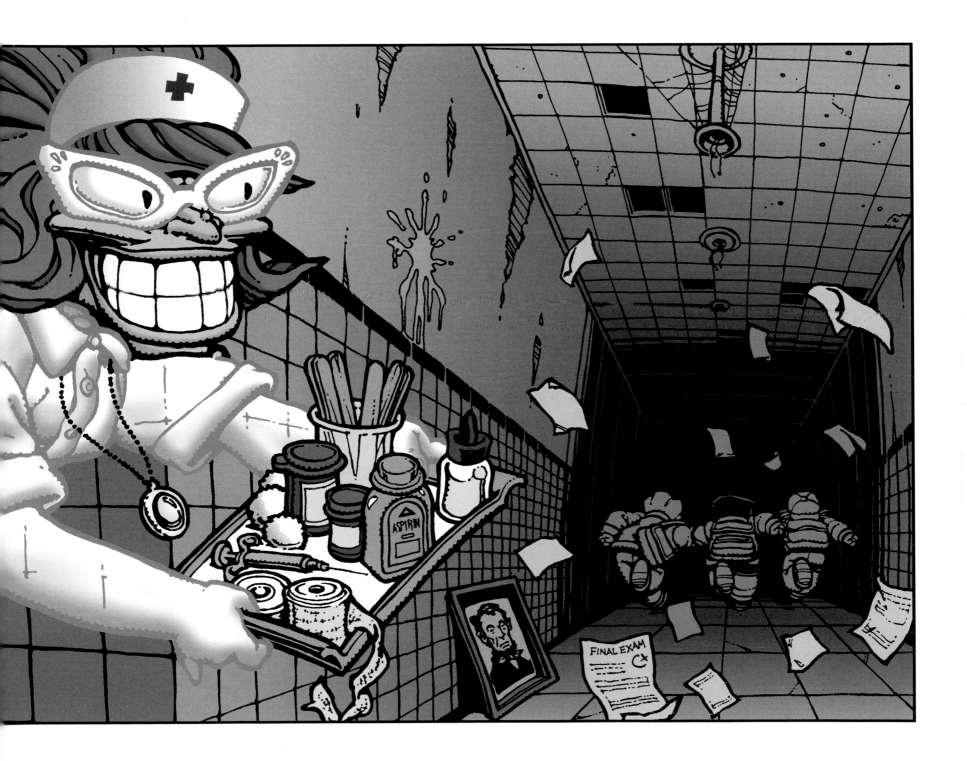

a! You think you can get away?" snarled Russ, the crazy custodian. "Into the basement and be quick about it!"

With a *whoosh* of his gigantic, disgusting push broom, he forced us back the way we came.

Yikes! Lurking right around the corner was the ghost of Principal Strong himself! And behind him loomed an open door . . .

. . . to the basement.

We stopped, frozen in our tracks.

"Get down those stairs, you little hoodlums!" he thundered. Then, smiling far too sweetly, he added, "Don't worry, no one will hurt you . . ."

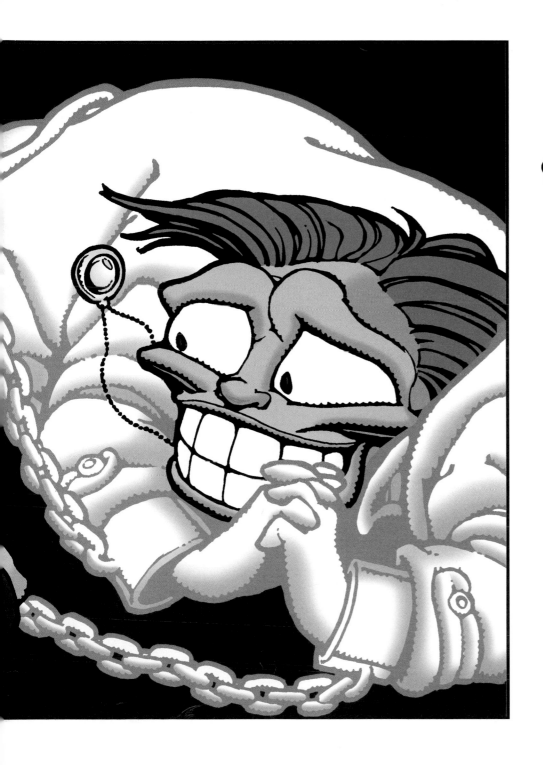

ith that, we dashed like mad dogs back down the main hallway, screaming all the way, searching desperately for an escape.

The chained student caught up and floated along beside us, begging us to stay. "Come on back, you guys," he moaned, "it's *fun* in the basement!"

t last, we made our way out.

To our surprise, there was Dallas. Delbert and Kendall immediately recovered and began to tease him.

"What's the matter, wimp?" they jeered. *"Just couldn't take it,* could you? A little too *scary* for you, *wasn't it?"*

Dallas just smiled and said, "Yeah, I guess so. You guys are *really* brave!"

ight fell as Dallas and I headed home.

I asked where he'd been, and he said, "Oh, just hangin' around."

"By the way," he said, "you dropped this . . ."

. . . and he calmly handed me my Uncle Stanley's mask.